The Legend of EL Dorado

A Latin American Tale

Story and illustrations by Beatriz Vidal

adapted by Nancy Van Laan

ALFRED A. KNOPF  NEW YORK

A mi padre,
que me contó cuentos
y me indicó el camino de El Dorado

—B. V.

For my brother Philip and my sister Helen,
and my two other children, Jan and Hannah

—N. V. L.

THIS IS A BORZOI BOOK PUBLISHED BY ALFRED A. KNOPF, INC.

Text copyright © 1991 by Nancy Van Laan
Illustrations copyright © 1991 by Beatriz Vidal
All rights reserved under International and Pan-American Copyright
Conventions. Published in the United States by Alfred A. Knopf, Inc.,
New York, and simultaneously in Canada by Random House of Canada
Limited, Toronto. Distributed by Random House, Inc., New York.

Library of Congress Cataloging-in-Publication Data
Van Laan, Nancy. The Legend of El Dorado
/ by Nancy Van Laan ; illustrated by Beatriz Vidal.   p.   cm.
Summary: A retelling of the Chibcha Indian legend
about how the treasure of El Dorado came to be.
ISBN 0-679-80136-7 (trade) ISBN 0-679-90136-1 (lib. bdg.)
1. Chibcha Indians—Legends. 2. Indians of South America—
Colombia—Guatavita, Lake, Region—Legends. 3. El Dorado—Juvenile
literature. [1. Chibcha Indians—Legends. 2. Indians of South
America—Legends. 3. El Dorado.] I. Vidal, Beatriz. ill.
II. Title   F2270.2.C4V36   1990   398.2'089982086146   [E]—dc20   89-7998   CIP AC

Manufactured in Singapore   10 9 8 7 6 5 4 3 2 1

A Note About the Story

I first encountered the mythical El Dorado in the stories my father told me when I was a child in Argentina. I can still hear his voice, whispering with mysterious inflections tales of men in search of magical cities of gold, whose people lived forever. Although the exotic flavor of those myths remained with me, it wasn't until much later that I came across the original source. Having found El Dorado once again, I realized I had uncovered a rich and fascinating treasure, and I was eager to paint the legend.

I felt that Nancy Van Laan, with whom I had successfully collaborated on *Rainbow Crow* (a Lenape Indian legend), had the right poetic voice for the story. Happily, El Dorado captured her imagination too, and she agreed to retell it. Together we discussed the version that would be most appealing to children without losing the romantic, tragic flavor of the tale.

The name "El Dorado" (literally "The Gilded Man," whose body was covered with gold dust) comes from the account of an Indian in Colombia, as told in the chronicles of the conquistador Sebastián de Benalcázar, dated 1541, upon which this adaptation is based. The Spanish conquistadors heard many such wondrous fables from the natives when they arrived in the New World in the first half of the sixteenth century. Over the years El Dorado grew to symbolize everything related to the quest for gold in the unexplored jungles of South America; there came to be as many El Dorados as there were versions of the tale. For centuries the legend was the favorite gossip among royalty and soldiers, spurring their adventurous spirits. And for those who went on the quest and even gave their lives to satisfy their lust for gold, it became as frustrating as the torture of Tantalus. El Dorado was always elusive, always beyond the next mountain or the next river. It became a myth and a dream: at times a gilded man, at times a golden city, at times a gleaming kingdom.

Paradoxically, the mysterious El Dorado was indeed found…but the Spaniards never knew it. It was found in the enormous amounts of gold that the Indians extracted from the earth and shaped with the most admirable sense of aesthetics. It was found in the beliefs and the sacredness of the Indian's way of life.

As bits and pieces of the treasure are recovered, the real El Dorado begins to unfold, the one that has lain dormant, waiting to be discovered, not by conquerors but by true seekers. For El Dorado is much more than the physical and glittering gold: it is that inner city of the spirit, which one needs the utmost purity of heart to enter.

Beatriz Vidal

Lake of sadness, full of gold,
Now your legend must be told.

Long ago, before any creature lived on Earth, the pale Moon, blinded by the light of the Sun, shed a single tear. Round like the Moon, the teardrop became Lake Guatavita, the holiest of all lakes.

The Chibchas were the first to see Lake Guatavita, and they honored it as a gift from the god of the Moon. But there were also those that feared the moon-shaped lake. They believed that a mighty serpent slept beneath its surface, and that whoever touched the strange water and woke it would never return.

The Chibchas' king lived with his wife and daughter in a splendid palace by the lake.

Tall mountains surrounded them, full of emeralds and green like the sea. Dancing streams circled them, full of gold and yellow like the sun. The emeralds and gold were used to make armor, ceremonial masks, and beautiful jewelry.

Early one morning, the queen and princess were walking through the forest when the little girl saw Lake Guatavita shimmering between the trees. Before her mother could stop her, the princess had rushed to the water's edge and rippled its surface with a stick.

The sun dipped behind the trees. Frightened, the queen tried to pull her daughter away, but it was too late. On the water's cool surface a shadow appeared, luring them to stare into the depths below—and into the ruby eyes of a dazzling emerald serpent.

Almost at once the sun's rays returned and erased the vision from the lake. The queen, shaken, led her daughter back to the safety of the village.

But later, when the queen described what she had seen to the king, her fear disappeared. "It is a beautiful serpent," she said. "Its scales are made of emeralds, its eyes are red as rubies, and its glance is so entrancing I long to be with it forever!"

The king was alarmed and warned his wife never to go near Lake Guatavita again.

But that evening a nightmare woke the queen. From out of the
shadows two ruby-red eyes gleamed. "Come with me," they
seemed to say.

And just before daylight, holding her sleeping child, the queen
followed the strange red eyes to Lake Guatavita.

When the king woke to find his wife and child gone, he ordered his men to search the kingdom. But secretly he knew that the serpent of the lake had cast its dreadful spell.

At last the king and his warriors approached the lake. As he drew close, the king cried out—he thought he saw the queen and princess mirrored in the dark water. But a strong gust of wind shattered the stillness and the image vanished.

Then slowly the queen's royal belt and the princess's cape rose to the surface. Knowing that he could not reach for them, the king turned away.

The king returned to the village alone. No longer was he happy—his wife and daughter, like stones upon the water, were gone. No longer was he mighty—his strength and wisdom, like faint dreams, were forgotten. And no longer were the Chibchas content—their ruler, like a withered leaf, was crumbling.

Soon other tribes would overcome them. Soon all their land would be gone. Soon all their treasures would be taken. *No! No! No!* the Chibchas cried. This could not happen!

Uncertainly, the priests of the tribe met to decide the fate of their kingdom. "We must find a way," they agreed, "to strengthen our king."

The high priest raised his hand to speak. "The moon will soon be full," he said. "We will gather by the lake and wait for the serpent to speak."

So on the eve of the full moon the Chibchas surrounded Lake
Guatavita. The moon rose slowly, creating a circle of light on the
quiet water.

The sacred fire burned brightly, and the drums beat softly as
dancers moved to the rhythm. "*Chi-cha, chi-cha,*" the Chibchas
chanted, and the high priest prayed to the gods.

Suddenly the moon slipped into the mist and a fierce wind rose. No more shadows, all was darkness. Waves thundered across the black water, roaring a message from deep below.

When the mist cleared, again the moon formed a circle of light in the center of the lake.

"The serpent has spoken," the high priest said to the king.

"Your wife and child are happy in its palace."

"But what must I do to be with them?" the king asked. The lake swallowed up the moon's shadow and once more the waves roared.

"Your hour has not yet come," the high priest said. "You must rule your kingdom wisely. And in time you will be reunited with your family."

Instantly the lake grew calm and the gentle warmth of the full moon embraced them. The king went back to the village and ruled his kingdom with renewed strength. And once more the Chibchas were peaceful and content.

But the king feared that the serpent might forget its promise. So to remind and honor it, the king and his people created a special ceremony.

Once each year the Chibchas anointed their king with fragrant oils, then covered his body with gold dust. He became El Dorado, "The Gilded Man," for he was golden like a god. Seated upon his throne, the king was carried to the edge of Lake Guatavita.

At sunset, on his royal raft laden with emeralds and gold, he drifted across the water while a chorus of flutes and voices filled the air. When the raft reached the middle of the lake, the music stopped.

The king called upon the serpent to guard his wife and child.
And as he chanted his prayers he threw his treasures one by one
into Lake Guatavita.

When nothing was left, the king himself plunged into the water, offering the golden dust that covered his body. And a circle of gold, round like the moon, rose to the surface and glittered in the slender rays of the setting sun. Amid the shouts of his people, the triumphant king swam back to shore.

Year after year this ceremony was performed, until at last the serpent kept its promise. As the serpent's ruby eyes beckoned him to follow, the king sank. And down below he was reunited with his lost family.

Each new king repeats this ritual so that the serpent of the lake will keep his kingdom safe. But to this day the treasures of El Dorado remain hidden, locked in the depths of Lake Guatavita.